Smart Little Mouse

Children's book

ELENA PANKEY

Smart Little Mouse

Children's book

ELENA PANKEY

ISBN: 978-1-952907-37-1

No copyright infringement is intended

Contents

Sunny Garden

Once upon a time, one mouse family lived nearby the house in the beautiful hillside garden. That fenced garden was near the big house, and grew refreshingly casual, providing food and shelter for wildlife.

There were many living creatures happily playing together in the fragrant garden. The owners of the house tried to work hard to make it even more beautiful and healthy. The paved front yard was facing the west, and only tall cypress trees protected the front yard from the hot sun.

***

The love of gardening is a seed once sown that never dies.

Mouse Family

One day Mother Mouse had new babies, and was caring for them from the morning to the evening, and they grew very fast. At night, the Mother Mouse had to go to get some food for them.

While she was absent, she hired a nanny to watch them, to sing a lullaby, and put them to beds. But little children did not like the nannies songs. Every night they asked for a new nanny with the different voice and new songs. All nannies were singing in their natural voices, which their own children liked very much.

One night it was a goose nanny, another night it was a goat nanny, third night it was a chicken nanny. So, the goat nanny was singing as all goats do by just bleating: "Be-ee-be"!

The chicken nanny was crowing like all chickens do: "Ku-kare-ku"! The goose nanny was hissing like all geese hiss: "Shee-e-she"!

But the children of the Mother Mouse did not enjoy such kind nannies voices. They felt that such voices were too rude, or too lode, or too freighting to them.

One night Mother Mouse was not at home and all her babies were weeping and crying: *"We won't sleep alone! We want a good nanny to put us to sleep"*.

Then, the Little Smart Mouse wanted to help them. So, he invited a cat to sing a lullaby to his brothers and sisters.

The cat tenderly hummed, and all mice liked his voice and quickly fell asleep.

Then, the hangry cat started to plan his feast. But

the Little Smart Mouse hid in the hole, and yelled from there to his brothers and sisters: *"Get up and run away. The big cat will have you for his dinner"*!

When the Mother Mouse came back home, she did not find her children. She concerned about what happened, and asked everyone around if they saw what happened.

Only observant dogs Tuzik and Sonia described the night adventure and how her children escaped from the hungry cat. The Mother Mouse was grateful for the

good news, and called her relatives to go to look for her children.

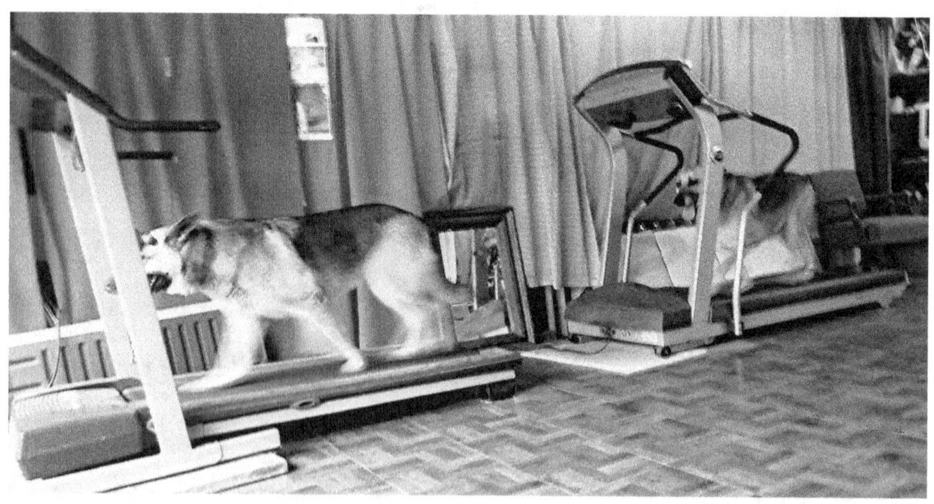

Observant Dogs

The owners of the house had two intelligent dogs Tuzik and Sonia. The dogs listened to the owner very attentively, knew many words, and tried to do everything they were asked in order to make the owners happy. Every dog had his personal comfortable house, and they guard and protect everything around.

But during the hot weather, they did not want to hunt, and just were lying down on the patio, while listening to the source of the sounds. However, since the dogs were very observant, they knew what's going around, and saw how the mice escaped the cat.

***

In one incredibly hot summer in California, even under the umbrellas of the front yard was no relief.

After the breakfast dog Tuzik tried to hide in the cool garage, and Sonia went to the garden to stay on the grass under the oak trees. The dogs knew that it was very useful for them to eat medical herbs, which they found there.

In addition, their loving mistress Alenushka got each of them a huge lounge on the porch. Sometimes, after the games and swimming, Tuzik and Sonia liked to rest in the hammock or lounge. Moreover, every dog had his own pool to cool down after their exercises on the trade mills. With such wonderful care, the dogs felt

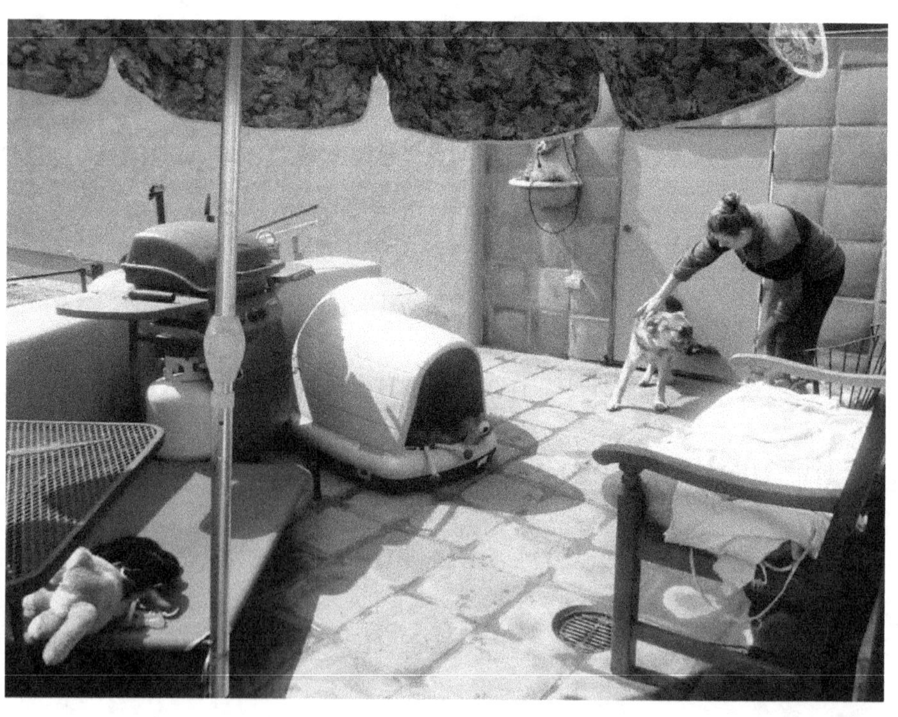

good about their lives and their owners. Dogs thought that their purpose was to make everybody happy. They waved the tail, and tried to kiss everybody.

In the very hot days, some other living creatures of the courtyard tried also to stay in the shade of the umbrellas. They were hiding and in the grass or behind the dogs houses. Sometimes when the house door would be open for a minute, the wonderful coolness of the fans poured out onto the hot tiles of the sunny yard.

***

Pleasant House

The Little Smart Mouse was sitting in the front yard trying to hide from the heat. He was not an experienced mouse, and seeing that there were no dogs nearby, he ran onto the porch.

When the house door was open, the mouse with no hesitation rushed into the saving coolness of the house.

Suddenly, finding himself in an unknown corridor, the frightened and stunned Little Smart Mouse immediately hid under a table.

For some time he sat there quietly, trying to understand where he is and how dangerous it is for him. However, after a while the Little Smart Mouse felt severe hunger.

He began to run around the huge house looking

everywhere for some food. But the floor in the house was often washed, observing perfect cleanliness, and there were practically not even small crumbs anywhere. But several times he came across the owners of the house and immediately slipped under the stove in the kitchen. The owners were surprised to see strange presence of a scurrying Little Mouse, who so openly ran around.

The hostess exclaimed: *"Look, the little mouse is running around here like he is in a park"?* And she left to set tempting mouse traps.

***

Soon the Little Smart Mouse understood that it was incredibly dangerous to run around someone else's property. He wanted, by all means, to find a way to the freedom, and tried again his luck in search of the hole to outside. Suddenly he smelled pleasant aroma of an incredible delicacy. He cautiously approached the yellow plate and started to think how to get that delicious food without troubles. But he remembered the story of his Mother Mouse told him about the danger of the delightful and free food on the unknown plate.

Surviving Story

Once the Mouther Mouse told her children how people helped her to escape the deathly danger of the trap. It was long time ago, when in one hot day she got in the house. But the owner of the house found her in a trap, was sorry for her and began saving the mouse. He gently covered the mouse's head with a towel. Then, he placed his hand over the mouse body to hold her in one spot. Then, he poured a little vegetable oil onto

the trap where the mouse was stuck, and avoiding the mouse body. After that, the man took a cotton swab and massaged the oil into the glue. Eventually, the glue began to loosen and the mouse was able to release itself from the trap. After all that work, the mouse needed to rest. So, the master of the house put some water near her, and covered her with the container. Later, the mouse was taken outside to the garden.

***

The Little Smart Mouse did not want to take any chance and beg for this life if he would get into the trap. Besides being very talented, he knew how to count and analyze things around him. He calculated the distance to the edge of the trap before thanklessly running into it. In order to get to the edge of the food and not stuck into the tarp, he needed to jump as hard as he could. So, he did it.

He luckily landed not in the dangerous middle of that trap, but very close to the delicious peanut butter left in the sticky mousetrap. The Little Smart Mouse quickly ate this delicacy, and immediately felt much better. He thought that *"the morning is wiser than the evening,"* and he might stay overnight in this place. But then the words of his wise Mother Mouse sounded:

"If you ever would get into a people's house, do not eat or drink anything for three days. Try to get out of there, no matter what. But if you get tempted and taste something incredibly delicious on the "sticky" place; try to lick the glue out of your pawns and jump out of it".

***

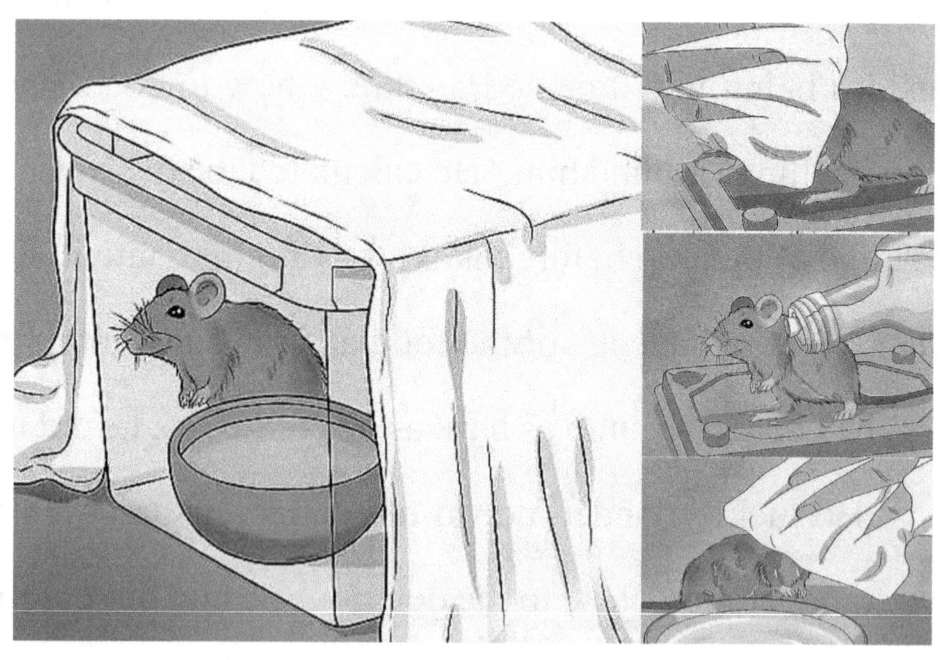

Happy Effort

From the moment when the Little Smart Mouse disappeared in the people's house, his many relatives started to search for him. At night, the owner of the house heard the fuss of the mouse on the mousetrap and came to look at him. Suddenly the Little Smart Mouse saw a huge mistress in front of him and was scared even more. But this person was his only salvation, because only the man could help him to escape.

The Little Smart Mouse took all his courage as the last chance for freedom, and shouted with all his might: *"Help! Save me! Don't let me die here"!* And his eyes sparkled and begged for help.

For most men, such a creature is just a dirty mouse that spreads infection everywhere. But for the owner of the house, this thin voice of the Little Smart Mouse sounded desperate and the mouse's plea did not go unnoticed. Alenushka carefully took the mouse outside and put him on a high post, away from dogs.

The Little Smart Mouse was delighted with the fresh air. He knew that only freedom and happiness smelled like that. He looked around and realized that only one place on the mousetrap was not so sticky. This place still had traces of peanut butter. He started to lick his front legs for a long time, trying to clear them of the terrible glue. Then he stretched out and put his clean paws in the place of the peanut butter, where the glue did not hold him.

At that time mice relatives were still looking for the children of Mother Mouse. They smelled the Little Smart Mouse nearby and ran to his aid. His Mother Mouse scrambled onto the pole and began to help her child to get rid of the glue.

The love and support of his family gave more confidence and strength to exhausted and scared Little

Smart Mouse. He pulled himself up, caught on the clean edge of the glue, and pulled away from the place that held him so tightly. Then, he felt the wonderful feeling of the long-awaited freedom, and with great relief run away. All his relatives ran away with him to celebrate the miraculous release of the Little Smart Mouse.

During that night the dogs in the front yard saw how the mice relatives helped him to escape. They understood their hard effort. So, the dogs did not bark, and did not try to hunt them all, as they usually would do. The dogs loved that story about the Little Smart Mouse and his Family.

***

THE END

About Author

The author, Elena Pankey has created many fascinating books in Russian and English, and published them in Europe and America. Among them, it is worth noting several funny books about the lives of cats and dogs, about monuments to beloved animals. Also, her wonderful books about Argentine tango or about the famous Ukrainian artist Valeria Bulat cannot be ignored. Moreover, her historical and biographical trilogy about Gelendzhik, memories of her hometown and people who lived there in the 1950-1990s are unusually interesting.

The author has many years of experience in various fields of education, literature, theater, dance, cinematography. She especially enjoyed the work of a tour guide, traveling with tourists around Russia and the Baltic states. She also shared with people her love of art and knowledge of the museums and palaces of St. Petersburg. After several marriages, she found her true happiness in California.

***

Proverbs

Two cats and one mouse, two women in one house, two dogs to one bone, will not agree long.

***

Three things it is best to avoid: a strange dog, a flood,

and a man who thinks he is wise.

***

Don't make a mouse of yourself, or else you will

be eaten by cats.

***

A cat is a lion to mouse.

***

It is little honor to the lion to seize the mouse.

***

It's a poor mouse that sits on the sack and doesn't

gnaw.

***

The cat's play is the mouse's death.

***

What is sport to the cat is death to the mouse.

***

No house without a mouse, no barn without corn, no

rose without a thorn.

***

New Books

STRONG LUST FOR LIFE
Alenka's Tales
ELENA PANKEY

WHERE FEARS ARE HIDING
ALENKA'S TALES
BOOK 5
ELENA PANKEY

Thirst for Life
Alenka Short Stories
ELENA PANKEY

Learning To Fly
AND STORIES
Alenka's Tales
Book 4
ELENA PANKEY

Copy Rights

978-1-952907-37-1